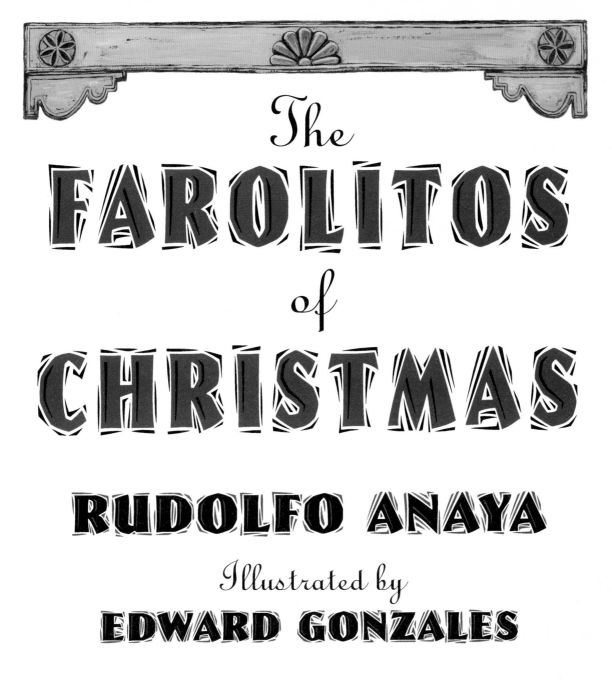

The
FAROLITOS
of
CHRISTMAS

RUDOLFO ANAYA

Illustrated by

EDWARD GONZALES

Hyperion Books for Children

New York

For Kristan
—R.A.

To my daughter Alicia,
my granddaughter Zia Elena,
and Consuelo,
with love
—E. G.

Text copyright © 1987, 1995 by Rudolfo Anaya.
First published in 1987 by *New Mexico* magazine.
Illustrations © 1995 by Edward Gonzales.
All rights reserved.
Printed in Hong Kong by South China Printing Company Ltd.
For information address Hyperion Books for Children,
114 Fifth Avenue, New York, NY 10011.

FIRST EDITION
1 3 5 7 9 10 8 6 4 2

Library of Congress Cataloging-in-Publication Data

Anaya, Rudolfo A.
The farolitos of Christmas / Rudolfo Anaya ; illustrations by
Edward Gonzales — 1st ed.
p.   cm.
Summary: With her father away fighting in World War II and her
grandfather too sick to create the traditional *luminarias,* Luz helps
create *farolitos,* little lanterns, for their Christmas celebration
instead.
ISBN 0-7868-0060-7 (trade) — ISBN 0-7868-2047-0 (lib. bdg.)
{1. Christmas—Fiction.   2. Mexican Americans—Fiction.
3. Grandfathers—Fiction.   4. New Mexico—Fiction.}   I. Gonzales,
Edward, date. ill.   II. Title.
PZ7.A5186Far   1995
{Fic}—dc20   94-48073

Luz hurried down the dirt road toward the *pueblo* where her friend Reina lived.

"Caw, caw," the black crow called from the bare branches of the cottonwood tree.

To Luz, his cry sounded like "Cold, cold."

"Yes, Mr. Crow," she said to the large black bird. "It is a cold morning. And only three days till Christmas."

Luz lived in the village of San Juan in northern New Mexico. Across the road lay the pueblo where Reina lived.

Except for a few children on their way to school, the streets of the village were empty. Smoke rose from the chimneys into the cold December air.

Perhaps it will snow for Christmas, Luz thought, looking at the tall peaks of the Sangre de Cristo Mountains. Dark clouds were forming on the blue majestic mountaintops. Luz snuggled her chin down into her wool scarf and walked on.

At the village grocery store, Luz stopped to look in the window. In the center stood a cardboard figure of Santa Claus.

"Qué bonito," she said aloud.

Her grandfather, who spoke only Spanish, called Santa "Santo Clos."

"Is Santo Clos real?" Luz had asked her grandfather one day.

"Oh yes, he's real." Abuelo winked. "He comes with his bag full of presents for the children. And the *pastores* come to adore and sing to the Santo Niño."

"I love the pastores." Luz smiled.

"They are an old tradition," Abuelo said. "On Christmas Eve some of the people of San Juan dress like shepherds and perform a play that shows the journey of the first shepherds to the birth of Jesus. Our pastores come down the road on their way to church, and they stop to sing in front of the house with the brightest *luminarias*."

"And that's our house!" Luz said happily.

"*Sí*. We place the piñon logs in small stacks from our door to the road. On Christmas Eve, we light the luminarias for the pastores, and they stop at our house and sing. Then we invite them in to eat *posole, tamales,* and *biscochitos*."

Abuelo had lit the luminarias every Christmas Eve since Luz could remember. Now he was sick with a terrible cold, and the doctor wouldn't permit him to work outside. There would be no luminarias this Christmas. The pastores would not stop to sing at Luz's house.

Luz crossed the road and entered the pueblo. Reina stood waiting in front of her adobe house.

"Hurry," Reina called. "We don't want to be late! Today we decorate the Christmas tree at school. Isn't that exciting!"

"Yes," Luz nodded. "We don't have a Christmas tree at home."

"We usually go to Taos Pueblo to dance and visit relatives on Christmas," Reina said, "but this year my father said we could stay home and have our own tree. Can you come over and help me decorate it?"

"Oh yes," Luz answered.

"My father will cut a tin star for the top of the tree."

Reina's father was a tinsmith in the pueblo. Her mother was a weaver.

"Is your father coming home?" Reina asked.

The country was at war, and Luz's father had joined the army. A month ago they had received a telegram with the news that he had been wounded and was in the hospital.

"We don't know if he will be home in time for Christmas," Luz said. She looked at her friend.

Tears filled her eyes. She turned and ran into the school so Reina wouldn't see.

At the end of the school day, Luz took out a tattered calendar from her desk. She had kept it since her father went away, and each day she crossed out the day gone by. Today she made an **X** over December 22.

She and Reina walked home from school. Reina's mother gave Luz *oshá*, an herb to make a tea that would help Abuelo. She also sent a loaf of warm bread she had just baked in the *horno*.

At home, Luz's mother was baking biscochitos, the traditional Christmas sugar cookie. The kitchen smelled delicious.

Abuelo sat napping in his big chair near the stove. The cat lay quietly on his lap.

"Luz, I'm glad you're home. How was school?" Mamá asked.

"It was fine," Luz said and took off her jacket. "We decorated the Christmas tree, and we sang 'Silent Night.' Then we exchanged presents. How is Abuelo?" She looked at her grandfather.

"He's feeling better today," Mamá replied.

"Reina's mother sent some oshá," said Luz.

Mamá made tea, and when it was ready Luz took a cup to her grandfather. She touched his arm.

"Abuelo, I'm home."

Abuelo opened his eyes. "Luz, *mi'jita*. I'm glad to see you. I fell asleep. I was dreaming, and in my dream I saw the pastores coming to our home. I saw Bartolo, the lazy shepherd, and I heard Gila singing. I saw San Miguel, the archangel, leading the pastores to the manger. And I saw the Devil trying to upset everything. That Demonio tries to tempt everyone, but San Miguel drives him away."

"What a beautiful dream!" Luz said and kissed her grandfather's cheek. She handed him the cup of tea and sat next to him. When she was by his side, she didn't feel sad anymore.

Abuelo sipped the tea. "Ah, this is better than the doctor's medicine," he said. "With this tea I will get well. Soon I will feel strong enough to cut the piñon. I promised the Santo Niño that I would light the luminarias for my son's safe return. I must keep my promise."

Luz knew that a promise to the Santo Niño had to be kept by the person who made it. That was why her grandfather would not accept help in cutting wood.

In the evening dusk, Luz walked to Reina's house. Reina's father had cut a small pine tree in the mountains. Luz and Reina tied popcorn chains and strings of brightly colored yarn on the tree. Reina's mother put a white wool blanket around the bottom of the tree to look like snow. Reina's father placed the tin star on the top of the tree.

When they finished, they stood back and admired their work.

"Our first Christmas tree!" Reina cried.

"On Christmas morning, the pueblo will dance the Deer Dance," Reina's mother said.

"And on Christmas Eve, the pastores," Luz said.

"Your grandfather always lights the luminarias," Reina's mother smiled. "It's the most beautiful part of Christmas."

"But because my abuelo is sick the doctor won't let him do any hard work," Luz said sadly. "He can't cut piñon logs. He can't even cut wood for the stove."

"Does that mean there won't be any luminarias?" Reina asked.

Yes, Luz thought, this year there won't be any luminarias.

There was no school the following day. Luz helped her mother clean the house and prepare the *masa* for the tamales. When all was done Luz sat with her dolls near the window.

"Why so sad, mi'jita?" Abuelo asked.

"Because Papá isn't home, and we won't have the luminarias," Luz replied.

"We will!" Abuelo said. "I feel better today. I can chop the wood."

He put on his jacket and went outside to the woodpile. He picked up the ax and tried to chop the huge logs, but it was no use. He was too weak, and his cough returned.

"Abuelo, come in the house!" Mamá insisted. She would not let him stay out in the cold.

Reina came in the afternoon, and she and Luz set up a *nacimiento* that had been in the family a long time. The figures of the baby Jesus in the cradle, Joseph, Mary, the three wise men, and the animals were carved from piñon wood. Afterward, Reina and Luz decorated the sill of the kitchen window with small candles.

"We will light them on Christmas Eve," Mamá said. "Maybe the pastores will stop when they see them."

"I think not," Abuelo said. "If there are no luminarias, they will not stop. They will hurry to the church, where it is warm."

"Maybe we can place the candles outside," Luz said.

"Yes!" Reina cried.

"Do we have many candles, Mamá?"

"Oh, I have dozens," her mother answered.

"Then let's make a row of them!" Luz said. "From our door all the way to the road. The candles will be our luminarias!"

Mamá looked at Abuelo. He shook his head.

"Look," he said, and pointed out the window. "See those clouds in the mountains? That means a storm is coming. The wind will blow out the candles. That's why I have to use piles of piñon wood as luminarias. If the wind blows or if it snows, the pastores can still come and tell their story by the warmth of the fire. The people who come to watch the play can also keep warm. But candles? No. The wind would blow them out."

Again he shook his head and went back to the chair by the stove.

"Maybe we could put the candles in cans," Luz said. "Then the wind wouldn't blow them out."

"Then we couldn't see the light of the candles," Mamá said, and went back to work.

All afternoon, even after Reina went home, Luz thought and thought of what to do.

If only I had something to put the candles in, she thought. Then I could make a row of candles and light them for the pastores. Last night, when they talked, Abuelo had told her that she could help him keep his promise.

Just before dinner, Luz's mother called her.

"Please run to the store for sugar. I used all I had baking the biscochitos."

Luz put on her coat and mittens and ran down the road to the grocery store. When she entered, the radio was playing "White Christmas."

As the storekeeper poured the sugar into a brown paper bag, a light behind him made the sugar glisten like glittering stars.

The starlight can be poured into the bag, Luz thought. The bag will protect the candles and allow their light to be seen.

And she had dozens of bags at home that she had saved all summer to sell back to the storekeeper!

Full of excitement, Luz hurried home. Her heart was pounding. When she got home, she quickly emptied the sugar into her mother's sugar can.

"I can put the candle in the bag!" she exclaimed.

"But the wind will blow it away," Mamá answered.

"I can pour a cupful of sugar into the bag. That will hold it!" Luz said. Her heart beat faster. She ran to her grandfather.

"Abuelo, we can put the candles in the paper bags! That way they won't go out!"

"Yes," he smiled. The bag would protect the candle, and the light would shine through. Maybe Luz had found a way!

"We can put a candle in each bag and make luminarias!"

She handed Abuelo the bag and ran to get one of the small candles. "See, like this." She placed the open bag on the table and put in a cupful of sugar. Then she placed the small candle snugly in the sugar.

"Now we can light it," she said. She felt her heart racing.

"But we can't waste all that sugar," Mamá said.

"Wait! Let's try it," Abuelo said. "If it works, we can use sand in the bag, not sugar."

He took a match from his pocket and lit it by scratching it with his thumbnail. Then he lit the candle inside the bag. It sputtered, then glowed brightly. The three stood looking at the warm glow of the candle. The light seemed to dance inside the bag.

"It looks like a little lantern," Abuelo said. "You have made a beautiful *farolito*. That's what it is, a farolito. Will it stay lit outside?"

Luz tenderly picked up the bag with the lighted candle and walked out into the night. She placed the bag near the road. In the dark, the candle in the brown paper bag glowed brightly. It didn't go out!

Luz ran back to her mother and Abuelo. The three stood huddled at the door, looking at the farolito that shone in the dark night.

"Oh, it is beautiful," Mamá said.

"Imagine a hundred of them," Abuelo said. "All along the path to the road, on top of the adobe wall, shining to light the way for the pastores."

"I have dozens of bags," Luz said.

"And I have dozens of candles," her mother said.

"And I can bring sand from the arroyo," Abuelo said.

They laughed and hugged each other.

"Tomorrow I'll tell Reina," Luz said. "She can help."

That night before she went to bed, Luz looked out the window. The little farolito she had made was still burning brightly. Tomorrow night was Christmas Eve. There would be a hundred farolitos lighting the way. Luz prayed her father would be home in time to share the joy.

The following morning Luz jumped out of bed before the sun rose. She hurried to help Abuelo light the wood stove to warm the house.

"You look happy, mi'jita," her grandfather said.

"I am happy," Luz answered. "I can hardly wait to tell Reina the secret. And you, Abuelo, how do you feel?"

He smiled. "I feel much stronger. I think it was the oshá tea. I'm ready to make farolitos."

Luz hugged him.

After breakfast Luz put on her coat and mittens and ran to
Reina's house. She told Reina the secret of the farolitos, then they
hurried to Luz's house to make them.

Abuelo went to the arroyo and brought back sand in a wheel-
barrow. Luz and Reina opened all the bags and put handfuls of
sand in each one. In the base of sand they placed a candle. When
they finished, they put the little bags all in a row, from the door to
the street. They even put bags along the top of Abuelo's adobe
wall.

Some of the boys from school stopped by.

"What are you doing with the bags?" one of them asked.

"We're going to catch falling stars," Luz answered.

"Ha!" the boys laughed. "Nobody can catch stars."

"Come tonight," Abuelo said with a twinkle in his eyes. "You'll
see."

Late in the afternoon, when they had finished setting up the
farolitos, Luz, Abuelo, and Reina went inside to drink hot chocolate. Now all they had to do was wait till it got dark to light the
candles.

That afternoon the people of the village went to visit and take food to the elders. They also went to the pueblo to visit their *vecinos*, the Indians.

Luz and Reina waited at the window. They watched the sun set and the first wisps of snow begin to fall. Soon it was dark, and the soft snow was falling like white feathers.

"It's time to light the farolitos!" Luz shouted.

"Yes!" Reina cried.

They looked at Abuelo. "Yes, it's time." He smiled.

Abuelo held the matchbox. Luz and Reina carefully went from bag to bag and lit each candle. Soon a hundred farolitos shone brightly in the dusk.

Then the pastores came down the road. They stopped to look at the farolitos glowing in the dark.

"The Star of the East," Gila, the shepherd girl, said. All the pastores agreed. The farolitos were the stars guiding them to Bethlehem.

Many of the villagers gathered around and listened to the pastores sing. Luz and Reina stood side by side, beaming with happiness. The light was reflected in their eyes. Abuelo stood by them, as happy as the children.

When the song ended, all the pastores and neighbors were invited into the house to eat. Abuelo served the posole spiced with hot chile. Mamá served biscochitos and hot chocolate for dessert.

"You did catch falling stars!" Abuelo said and put his arms around Luz and Reina. "Next year, every house will have farolitos."

Luz smiled. Everyone was happy. The children kept going to the window to look at the farolitos.

Luz, too, went to the window. She was glad she had helped her grandfather keep his vow to the Santo Niño.

Down the road Luz saw the evening bus stop in front of the grocery store. A man stepped down, and the bus drove away. Luz peered into the dark. The man walked stiffly, with a cane. He stopped in front of the house to look at the farolitos.

Luz recognized her father.

"Papá! Papá!" Luz cried, and ran out the door to greet him. He dropped his cane and swept her up in his arms.

"You're home," she cried, and hugged him. "Are you all right?"

"A little wound," he said, "but nothing to worry about. I'm so glad to be home. What's this?" He pointed at the farolitos.

"We made them today. Abuelo couldn't cut the wood for the luminarias, so we made farolitos."

"They're beautiful," her father said.

Mamá came running out of the house and hugged Papá joyfully. "I'm so glad you're home and safe!" she cried.

"*Gracias al Santo Niño*," Abuelo said, and embraced his son.

"Come inside," Mamá said. "You'll catch cold."

The neighbors greeted Papá. They were thankful he had returned safely. Now Abuelo's family was together again.

Then it was time for the procession to continue to the church. Everybody went out shouting, "Feliz Navidad! Feliz Navidad!"

Later that night, when Luz and her family returned from church, the farolitos were still glowing brightly. In the dark they shone like guiding lights, welcoming the family home.

"Farolitos de Luz," Abuelo said, "shining every Christmas, as long as there is love in our hearts."

GLOSSARY

abuelo	grandfather
biscochitos	traditional Christmas sugar cookies
farolito	small lantern
Feliz Navidad	Merry Christmas
gracias	thank you
horno	a round oven made from adobe bricks
luminarias	small bonfires of stacked wood
mamá	mother
masa	dough made of corn flour
mi'jita	my daughter, short for *mi hijita*
nacimiento	Nativity scene
oshá	an herb used for medicinal purposes
papá	father
pastores	shepherds
posole	a stew of hominy made with pork and chile
pueblo	a small village
qué bonito	how pretty
San Miguel	Saint Michael
Santo Niño	baby Jesus
tamales	chile and meat wrapped in corn dough and wrapped in corn husks
vecinos	neighbors